The Grocery Store On Lazaretska Street

Robert Buckeye

Spuyten Duyvil

New York City

ISBN 978-1-963908-09-1

For Peter Anastas

Introduction

Danek had come to Bratislava from America and Marina from the mountains of Eastern Slovakia. They were at a stage in their lives in which they asked themselves what was next. They saw, as they had not before, there was less time left. They met and got involved, not intending to, until at some point their lives spiral out of control and send them in different directions.

One day Marina begged for food at a grocery store. One day Danek could no longer take care of himself. One day she found out and went to him. He was not meant to be forgotten. He had not forgotten her. The story is told in *Nightfall* (2021).

The room Danek was in did not seem to be his, but it was where he was. At first, he'd only been there, but he was still there. He's here. That's all he knows. That he is not here, even if he was.

It was evening. He was with father. Father reached out to put a hand on Danek's shoulder but stopped himself. It was so much like father. He never expressed how he felt, but it would have meant so much to Danek if he had.

So much had happened since then. So much of it no longer there. Danek was aware that he had arrived at a place in the future, but he did not recognize anything. The time of his time was no longer there except as images out of the past brought them back.

Stay with him Melville said. Stay with him Walter Benjamin says. He feels them pushing him forward, without taking him along. Where he would go and what he would do no longer there.

He had come to Bratislava and does not remember leaving it, although the room he was in could be anywhere. The thought of Bratislava brought back the man at the Arab café. Old men who sat on benches remembering past loves. A man at the end of a bar finishing a beer he would never finish. In a bus after midnight.

Some nights Marina had said. Some nights. It is the first thing he remembers.

It was difficult for Danek to sleep. He would turn over only to turn back. He would jerk upright and think he saw something. He would wake up not knowing where he was.

The night he left Marina. The day he walked away from teaching. Weeks he had let go, turned away from, came rushing back. The years of Cleveland, Detroit and San Juan backed up against one another.

Once Marina left in the morning, Danek turned to his notebook. In the afternoon, he went back to it. It was what he did, but it got in the way, as it had before.

After dinner, Marina took the notebook from him. It was time to talk. He gave the notebook to her reluctantly. He would look for the notebook to make sure it was there before he said anything.

It would not be Danek who spoke to her, but a Danek who needed Marina to speak for him before he could speak to her. A dumb show of gestures that punctuated what words said as much as by what they did not say.

Her name was Lenka. She is the woman who had given Marina an apple and tomato. The woman who said the next time they would talk.

She remembered Marina standing outside the store, not sure what she would do, but knowing she had to do something. Did she know, even then, what their talk would be? Marina's breasts were firm. She had striking hazel-gray eyes. There's a room out back she had said. You can stay there. If she hadn't got it out, it would have been too late. Marina's breasts had stirred something in her.

That she would want a woman nearly fifty? A woman at least twenty years older? It made no sense, but nothing in her life had. It confused and disturbed her, but she had rushed into it, as if there were no tomorrow. As if she had been fucked into life.

She had married because that was what everyone did. Her husband provided her with a comfortable life, but once he lost his job, he began to beat her and chase other women. It was her, he said. If she had not....

Marina unsettled Lenka as much as she excited her. Lenka did not remember how it began. Whether it had been a certain glance, a smile, a hand on an arm, a word said in a certain way that meant more than it said. It did not matter. It was not meant to be, but she embraced Marina as if it did.

She soon realized that Marina could not refuse her. It gave Lenka a satisfaction she had not felt before, but she feared Marina would resent her, as much as she had come to resent her husband.

It soon became clear that she was as much a kept woman as she had been with her husband. She could pull away from Marina at any moment, say it was over, tell her that she was no longer needed in the store, had to leave, but knew when push came to shove, Marina would call the shots.

She feared what everyone would think if they knew. This was Slovakia. She would hear lesbian, dyke and bitch knowing it was her they meant. There would be graffiti on walls, letters sent, phone calls. Life would be more difficult than it had ever been.

She did not ask Marina about the man. There was no point in bringing it up. She needed Marina's help. If he did not cause any difficulty, she had no reason to worry. He might as well not be there.

You should have done something, she heard Marina

ask Matka, the Matovic girl, at the register. It's time you did something for yourself. Business had picked up since Marina began work in the store. Lenka went over to the cooler to stack bottles in it. She heard what Marina had said to the Matovic girl, as if she had not heard it before. It's time she did something for herself.

Marina did what she did because she could do nothing else. She needed Lenka as much as she needed Danek. If it had not been for Lenka, she would not have a roof over her head and Danek would not be with her. It was better, far better, than it could have been.

If this was all there was.
If this is how it would be.
If this is what it came down to.

That she would be with a man who at moments did not know she was there and desired by a woman she could not refuse. What had been done could not be undone. She had gone her own way, did what she wanted, whenever she wanted, but now.

She must have wanted Lenka to want her. It was a way of ensuring they had a place to live but she had not thought about it until one day she felt Lenka's hand on her shoulder. She remembered Johanna. It could have happened with Katka, but she had not been aware of it then. It just happened with Lenka, but Marina had to convince herself that she had not brought it about.

At some point Lenka would want more from her than she would give. She would see Danek to be in the way. She could be out on the street again. Her fear of the warehouse was always with her.

She saw Lenka take money out of the cash register and count it to make sure there was enough. She kept the store open after dark when she did not have to. Marina remembered Petya at the market. Pay me when you can she would say to one woman. If you need help, let me know, she will say to another. Marina will take over for me.

Marina had been taken over. If Lenka could no longer pay her, it would not stop her from putting Marina back out on the street, no matter how Lenka felt about her.

Danek made every effort to be with Marina, but she saw how difficult it was for him. He would laugh and smile, even if it was an effort for him. He did not say much.

He no longer knew what to say. His life had not come back. He asks her where it has gone. Who he is was not him. He wants Danek back. He wants him.

It will come back, Marina says. It will take time. She asks him if he remembers the man at the end of the bar the night they met. What she told him about her life in London. The apartment they lived in. The woman who peed behind bushes.

She takes his hand and holds it against her breast. Feel it, she says. The nipple of her breast hardens. He remembers. He remembers what he has always remembered.

She did not understand how Danek made it through the day. The room they were in was empty. There was no photo, any graffiti left on the wall, no flowers in a vase or cushion on a chair to suggest that anyone lived here. There was nothing to see out the window, but a building across the alley, a dumpster in front of it. Danek made no effort to leave the room.

One day Marina brought Danek an apple from the store to remind him that she was there. The next day she saw that Danek had moved the apple. She was curious. The following day she brought daffodils to see what he would do. He put them on top of her jersey which had been left on a chair but moved the apple so that it would be near the daffodils.

She wanted to see if he would continue to do what he did and left a broken vase she found in storage. He left the vase on the table but put the flowers alongside the vase. She brought him a beer bottle, a bracelet, and a spoon to see what he would do. Whatever had been lost, thrown away, no longer needed, not of any use. It was as if Danek was a boy again with toy soldiers.

The room was beginning to look like an attic or basement in which everything that was no longer used was dumped and forgotten. Danek would not let Marina take anything away, even when it became difficult to move around the room. Danek she would say, I live here too.

It made no sense, other than whatever sense Danek made of it. It was useless, a way to let time pass for Danek, no more than a game, but she suspected it was more than a game to Danek. This could not go on much longer, but she did not stop bringing him what she found.

There was little else in his apartment in America Danek said, but books, cds, lps, dvds, photographs and paintings. It might as well be a library and museum, he laughed. Now he made use of a beer bottle or child's cap, however he could. There was no going back to what his life had been, but what Marina brought him let him do what he could.

One day she did not see his notebook. It frightened her. The woman, who was sorry she had ever seen his notebook, felt as if she had lost something.

Lenka stands at the back door beside a stack of beverage crates, smoking. Her face is in shadow, eyes closed. It is difficult to tell her age. She no longer remembers how long she has worked in the store. She'd always been afraid that the next day would be her last.

There was no place she could go and no one to help her if the store closed. Her father was dead. Her brother in Germany. He has done well, business he says, but he never mentions what it is. She never hears from him. She doesn't know where her mother is. She'd run off with a plumber from Belgium after father died.

She had no life before she met Marina and there would be no life after Marina left. She tells customers how good a worker Marina was. That she is lucky to have her work in the store. It was difficult, so difficult to get good workers these days. She could not have found a better worker than Marina.

Look at you, Mrs. Dubrovnik says. She knew Lenka's husband but felt Lenka was a beaten woman long before she met him. She had married him so that he would take her away from the life she feared she would have, but he was not anyone's savior. There's this woman she hired. She's made a difference, but she did not see anything that would tell her what it was.

Marina makes everything easy, but not for Lenka. No one must know what is going on. Lenka does not believe it will last and thinks that their next kiss will be the last. It was unnatural—she won't use the words that describe it--but if she can't live without Marina, it cannot be wrong, as wrong as it is. She glances at Marina stacking tomatoes in a bin. That it must be kept secret makes it easier.

When Lenka hired Marina, she set up terms and conditions for work, but one day she had come across a magazine with obscene photos in it that her husband left. She could not stop looking at them, as awful as they were, as disturbing. A new world opened for her that she knew was awful but could not tear herself away from.

She laughed. She should set up terms and conditions for what they did. How far will she go? As far as Marina wants. Would she let Marina whip her? She would bare her ass. Burn her? She would hold out her hand. She will not give in to these fantasies, but she cannot stop herself from thinking of them. She is terrified by the woman she has become.

And then?

Lenka had never waited for then before.

Lenka goes into the store. She needs to order more pork, *bryndza*, onions. It is time she paid Marina more. She looked at the money in the cash register. It was not as if she bought Marina, but she had. She thought about it while she counted. Cunt? Five Euros. Ass? Three.

—Lenka, I need a break.

Marina went out the back entrance of the store with a cup of coffee and leaned back against a wall. A cat stopped to look at her before it went down the alley. Across the alley there was garbage on the ground next to a dumpster. Laundry had been hung on a line strung between windows in the building opposite. Her glance fixed absent-mindedly on the cat before it disappeared around a corner.

Danek did not demand anything of her, but he needed her. At moments he made no sense. He would say that he was in Detroit in front of a class and would look at her, as if she was a student. He would say that he was no longer there. It was not him she saw.

His mother had been an immigrant. Danek might as well have been one. He would say he did not belong with anyone, even family. He sees himself to be Mr. Jacob but does not explain who it is. One day Mr. Jacob was no longer there he said.

She never thought that it would last with Danek, but at some point--she did not know when it was--she needed him. After Johanna tried to kill herself, she had been dependent on Danek, but it had not been then. It must have been after he left her, and she was forced to live in the warehouse that it began to understand what it was. It was not something that could be explained.

She liked Lenka. She would not forget that Lenka had given her work and a place to live, but if she upset Lenka in any way, Lenka would put them out on the street. She was dependent on Lenka but had begun to understand that Lenka was increasingly dependent on her. That made it easier for her but also more difficult.

She had not betrayed Danek before, but felt she had to, if they were to get by. Sex with Lenka was not wrong, but why she did it was. She would not leave Danek, but she was afraid of what would happen if she left Lenka.

There was a window to be looked out of, but what Danek saw did not change. A two-story building across the alley. A dumpster outside it. A woman always at a window in the building opposite. The woman must see him as he saw her, but from her upper floor window she saw what he could not. The window had become for her a street through which she walked down each day he thought, but it was limited—confined—by what was out the window.

One day a man looked out the window instead of the woman. Danek did not see what he had just seen, as if it had not come into focus yet. For a moment he did not know where he was. As if, suddenly, there was no time anymore, no going forward and no going back, but it nevertheless pushed him forward, without taking him along. Drip by drip it settled into his consciousness.

He sees his father in the living room, *The Cleveland Plain Dealer* in hand. He points to an article on the front page. There had been a riot in Detroit. Bad things would happen if you left home, his father said. And bad things had happened to Danek in Detroit.

Then he sees Richard Nixon outside the White House walking among protesters, wanting to talk to them, to ask what they want, but he soon realizes that they won't listen. No one recognizes Nixon and he walks away.

Then he sees himself talking to a librarian in his neighborhood library that had books in Hungarian, Polish, Slovak and German. There is a man here she said. He spends all day reading German books at one of the tables. He takes notes. It's suspicious.

Then he sees his mother at the market on West 25th street, arguing about the price of tomatoes in Slovak or Hungarian, before moving on to onions. *Cibula* was the Slovak word for onion she told him. Old women in black with cloth bags moved slowly, haltingly, around them.

His notebook does not let him out of sight. It keeps him from doing something else, but from what he does not know. He no longer writes in it. An act of writing that speaks for itself.

Lenka ran a hand over the mattress where Marina had been, but, in a moment, turned over and lay face down where her hand had been. It brought back what the evening had been but reminded her that Marina was not there. She would wake one morning, and Marina would no longer be there.

It was late. She had to dress, make coffee, go into the store, begin the day, but she could not let go of how it felt to have Marina's hand on her breast. She had a good body, her husband said. He had a right to see it, but she never let him. When Marina unbuttoned her shirt, she had pulled back. It's all right, she said. I want to see you. You need to see me looking at you so that you will know what I see.

What they did was wrong, so wrong it could not be right, but she could not help herself. She stretched to ease her stiff back. Everyone would know. She would lose the store and be out on the street and have nowhere to live. Suddenly she saw a woman in a miniskirt and stiletto heels, her breasts visible and eyes not focused, leaning back against the wall of a building, waiting.

Someone was knocking at the front door of the store. There was always someone at the door first thing in the morning. Women in the neighborhood were up early to get pork, cabbage, paprika and beer to make dinner for their men. She dressed and for a moment glanced back at the bed. The knocking on the door louder, more urgent.

Mrs. Dubrovnik examined Lenka as if it would explain why the store had not been open. Her lips were pressed tightly together. Lenka forced herself to look at her. Was there pork tenderloin today? Mrs. Dubrovnik needed paprika. She had never seen Lenka look so well. Was the bread fresh? Something about the way she spoke irritated Lenka.

Lenka avoided looking at Mrs. Dubrovnik while she put port tenderloin, paprika and bread in a bag, but added a croissant, a favorite of Mrs. Dubrovnik. Marina had come into the store and seen Mrs. Dubrovnik leave. She glanced at Lenka and saw she was upset. They had to be as cautious during the day as much as they could be reckless at night.

One could, if.
And.
Yet there was.

—Not tonight, Lenka.

It was difficult to know what Danek thought the nights she was with Lenka, but he had not said anything. There had been times recently he had struggled to get an erection. It would become more of a problem, but it brought her closer to him. It was odd to think that Danek was her man, as if it had not been meant to be. Suddenly she saw old women sitting on benches far away in the mountains at the end of their lives. They had come to terms with what their lives had been.

Things had become more difficult with Lenka. That she liked her complicated matters. Her life had not been easy, but it did not stop her from helping Marina. If Lenka saved her, Marina's work in the store made things easier for Lenka. She had overcome her anxiety and fear about sex with Marina, but it disturbed Marina that she used Lenka to keep them off the streets.

On her way to their room, Marina saw herself walk out of the store, go down the street, see what was to be seen and wait for the night, wait for what the night would bring but found herself when she looked up at the door of their room. She waited a moment. She wanted to see Danek before he saw her, look at him.

Danek was sitting in a chair, his eyes closed, hands clasped tightly together. She went over to him and touched him on the shoulder. He opened his eyes and smiled when he saw her and reached out to her.

She sat on his lap, her arms around his neck and her head on his chest. Danek put his arms around her and pulled her closer to him. She rubbed her nose against his breast.

Her thoughts returned to the day she left the small village in the Tatra mountains, her mother on the porch not wanting her to go but knowing she must; to her first day in Bratislava, not knowing where she was or what she should do, but knowing that this was where she wanted to be; to her first days in London, Kamau saying it's been good, it's been damn good; to a bar in Bratislava where a man had come in. A man she wanted to see once she saw him.

Have a nice trip, sir, the woman at the baggage counter at Kennedy said, but Danek thought she meant someone else and looked behind him to see who it was. It must have been his trip to Bratislava. He had gone to so many places, as if he could never stay long in one place. Each trip, it seemed, in search of what was not there.

The longer he had been away the more his past came rushing back to become part of the present, as if it asked him to catch up to it; remember what was no longer there, what needed to be kept.

It was time—1968, 1970, 1989—as much as it was place—Detroit, San Juan, Indiana—that stayed with him. It's uncertainty. Contingency. The untimeliness of the times.

Danek noticed the woman at the window. She never missed a day. She had seen a world he imagined from how she smiled or why she turned away. Suddenly she put her hand against the window. For a moment she looked at what she had done, as if it surprised her. Danek did not know what to make of it. He thought of putting his hand against the window to feel what it had been like for her but did not want the woman to see him do it.

The day he put his hand on Cristina's pussy in the back of a garage behind their house came back to him. Two children discovering what they wanted before they knew what it was, writing a story they did not understand. He saw Julie Stevenson standing at the back of a crowd at his birthday. The hand of a woman on a window in a building in Bratislava, far from home, brought them back, as if they had not been lost.

He glanced around the room. A window, bed, table, sink, closet. The wallpaper faded. The mattress torn. A place where air and light did not enter. A place with no space. Its exit-lessness.

The woman looked out the window so that she would not have to see what her room was like Danek thought. She had brought back Cristina and Julie Stevenson for him, he thought, so that he would not have to see his room.

You have eyes. Tell me what you see.

Her face in the mirror surprised her. It was as if Lenka had never seen herself before. She put her hand on her cheek. Her finger traced her nose. She touched her lips remembering Marina's finger on them.

Her husband liked her full breasts and long legs, but as far as he was concerned, she might as well have been a picture in a magazine or an ad on tv. After they were married, he became obsessed by what she wore. It had to be a miniskirt, a blouse opened at the neck, heels, a different shade of lipstick.

She did what he asked, went along. It was what one did. It was what one did, if one did not want to live alone like Aunt Iveta. She liked to be seen with her husband. Svetlana would see her and wish she had a man. Her husband was pleased when other men saw her with him.

Then it stopped. As if in one moment he saw what other men saw. It made him defensive. He began to tell her that a married woman did not wear miniskirts, did not show their breasts. Men know what it meant. It irritated her. If a miniskirt attracted her husband, it would also attract other men, but she could not tell him that. It would make him angry, but how he felt angered her.

Once she began working in the store, a miniskirt was not good for business. Kids came into the store in whatever they felt like wearing, but most of her customers were housewives and the elderly. It was....

What was the word? She heard a woman say it on tv one night. Inappropriate. She smiled. If she ever said it, they would think it was someone else.

She remembered how she felt wearing a miniskirt, as if the wind caressed her thighs when she went down the street. The world was hers and not that of a man, mother or priest. A skirt that was less, much less, than what everyone saw and much more. She laughed. She had not thought that she was funny. She was not too old to wear one, but she knew what everyone would think.

She thought about how it felt and looked. Could she? She could. She imagined the look on Marina's face when she saw her standing alongside the bed in a miniskirt. She can't remember the last time she bought anything, but she should buy something now. It would show Marina that she did something for her.

Lenka washed her face but spread soap across the

mirror so that she could no longer see herself. She was not the woman she had seen in the mirror. She was not the woman her husband saw, not the woman Marina saw. She had seen her.

It is different with Marina in the store. She jokes, laughs, talks with everyone. Everything she does she does fast. Everything she says is an event. Everyone brightens up when she serves them.

She keeps at it, keeps at it, because if she doesn't keep at it, she will be overwhelmed by what she can't stop thinking about.

Danek was no longer there. She asks him how he is, but he does not say anything and glances out the window, as if it will tell him what to say. She asks him what he would like for dinner, she'll make pierogies specially for him, but he looks at her, as if he needs to be reminded that she is there before he says anything.

It was, it was he says, but he never says what it was. It was never anything more than it was, but he surprised her by saying it was a bar in Bratislava downhill from the train station. He had come in, sat at the bar and ordered a bourbon. The night had not begun, she thought, but she knew it had.

She had come to like Lenka. They worked alongside one another and helped one another out. They did not say much, but there was always a smile, a pat on the shoulder, a shrug they understood. She would always be indebted to Lenka. What happened would not last, but while it did, she held on, to keep what was left, however she could.

R ain. A slight drizzle. The sky was gray, a dark gray. The woman was not at the window in the building across the alley. Danek saw a child's cap on the floor under the sink. It had been....

A stoplight turned red and then back to green. Danek watched it for a long time. He told himself he should cross the street. He told himself he should wait. Then he told himself he should let the stoplight decide. He asked himself if it mattered. At what point did anything matter?

He hears someone ask what they slept under. It had been the teacher. He was in school. He had not been in school long. Danek knew what he slept under and without thinking said *paplon*. He had not said anything in class before and did not know why he did.

No one knew what a *paplon* was. The teacher asked him whether it was a quilt or a blanket. He did not know what to say. A *paplon* was a *paplon*. In the background he heard laughter. In a moment the teacher moved on to another subject to save Danek from further embarrassment.

When he asked his mother what a *paplon* was, she laughed. It was the Slovak word for quilt. Sometimes she used Slovak words when she spoke to him not aware that she had, as she did when she said *dobre noche* when it was time for him to sleep.

He made every effort to put that embarrassing moment behind him. Had it been the first touchdown he scored? A scholarship to college? His first book? His life flickered in front of him as if he waited for a stoplight to tell him what to do. After his refusal of a doctorate, his decision to stop teaching and even his divorce, he had not waited.

The language they did not understand in Cleveland had become the language they spoke in Bratislava. It was as if he had to return to the beginning to begin over.

Lenka watched utility poles go by the window of the train on its way to Zilina. Across from her a rosy-cheeked, overweight young mother held on to her child in her lap. An older, white-haired woman sitting next to Lenka knitted.

The train went north past Trnava and Trencin on its way to Zilina, but the utility poles rushing by the window seemed to be going south, taking Lenka back to Bratislava and to Marina.

Lenka no longer thought of Zilina as home. Her father had died when she was still a girl. Her brother left for Germany to get work. Her mother had run off to Belgium with a plumber. Lenka left as soon as she could. Only her sister remained.

She had not been back since she left and did not know what it would be like, but she had no choice. The funeral service for her mother would be in Zilina and Lenka, as the oldest child, would have to be there.

After Lenka got divorced her mother said she should come back home. Bratislava was no place for a single woman. It had been a mistake for her to go. Her Bratislava experiment was over, her sister laughed.

They said she was not too old to marry. They said

there were good men in Zilina. They said she did not want to be an old maid like Aunt Matka. Friends and neighbors remembered her. She could start over, as if her years in Bratislava had not happened.

They said they said they said. Without thinking she began counting utility poles as they went by. She was no longer the girl that they knew. She had left home angry. She knew what family and friends would be like. She did not know what they thought when she left home but could guess, but if they knew anything about her life in Bratislava now.

She heard the laughter of the child and the woman next to her say, he's a good child. Lenka had never been a good child and she was even less of a good child now. Her family would not understand why she would stay in Bratislava, but it must have something to do with them, if it did not have something to do with Bratislava.

The funeral would be a disaster and it had been. She sat in a church her mother never went to and heard a priest say things about her no one believed. She stood at the grave and saw grave diggers cover the coffin with dirt, as if they were burying her instead of her mother. At her sister's house afterward, she smiled, said what needed to be said. There were questions about her life in Bratislava she had not answered

Outside Trencin, the train stopped alongside the Vah River. Its water was sluggish, clogged with branches and logs, bottles and cans and whatever chemical companies downriver had dumped into the river. For a long while Lenka looked at the river.

Marina makes certain that the shelves are stocked, checks the cash register to make sure there is enough money, glances at what she must order today from the notes Lenka left, cleans the counter with a cloth. This and more this and even more she had to do before she opened the front door.

Mrs. Dubrovnik wants pork sliced thin, cabbage, onions and potatoes. Mrs. Pistanek complains about the price of milk and asks Marina if Lenka can do something about it. The Matovic girl takes a candy bar when she thinks Marina had not seen her. When she brings Mrs. Pistanek a quart of milk, she says she'll ask Lenka if Mrs. Pistanek can pay later. She's sorry her husband left.

Marina went over to the Matovic girl who was looking at magazines and held out her hand. She had taken things when she was a girl because she felt like it but had also taken things when she was desperate. She was not a thief any more than the girl was, but she would have to do something about it. The candy bar she said to the girl. The girl shook her head, denied she had taken anything. Marina held out her hand.

The girl gave the candy to Marina and tried to leave,

but Marina held her. You know what you've done. Ok? It's not a problem unless it becomes a habit. The girl would not look at Marina, but Marina waited until she did before she said you understand? She gave the candy back to the girl She watched the girl leave and asked herself if it had been her, would she let herself go?

After the Volko woman paid for a six-pack of beer, she laughed. I tell my man it's time he bought his beers, but he never listens. What can you do? A man's a man, but I love him. For a moment she glanced at Marina. Even when she said Marina there was a question in it. She would not be satisfied until she knew why Marina had come to work in the store.

Mrs. Dubensky remembered what it had been like at the market. She would bargain with a woman at a stall about the price of strawberries and corn. Today prices were fixed and set by someone who had no idea how strawberries and corn were grown.

They would not know that this year there had been too much rain and too many strawberries. That last year there was not enough rain and too little corn. Marina remembered Petya at her stall at the market. Even here, she thought, it was no longer what it had been.

By the middle of the afternoon, business had slowed. Marina leaned back against the counter and drank coffee. More tomatoes needed to be put in a bin and more beer in the fridge. She needed to get pork from the freezer. It would get busier at the end of the day.

She looked forward to spending the night with Danek. She thought of him holding her in his arms, rubbing her aching back, but suddenly, as if she saw it happen, she had taken his penis in her mouth.

Was that, this, then, it?

She rubbed her eyes, the hint of a smile on her face. She went over to make coffee. There was more to it now, ever more, even if it was less.

When Marina left, Danek looked at the door through which she had gone, as if it would tell him something. He did not know where she went, what she did, why. She always came back. They never asked one another what they did. It was a practice they had established early on in their relationship. This was different.

Should he know?
It would be better to let things lie.
Should he care?
He did not want to think about it.

Danek made no effort to leave the room, but one day he went up to the door and put his hand on its worn wood surface. One day he turned the doorknob but backed away from it once he had touched it. The door was there, the doorknob told him, to keep him from leaving.

Suddenly the day he was arrested in Detroit and put in jail came back to him. On his long walk past cells to his, one door had been shut and then another. One by one a long row of them closed, harsh noise of metal banging metal. The sound of them crisscrossing up and down the cell block, running ahead of him and then falling back. Then it was quiet.

These seconds remain fixed in his mind, echoing again and again, then silence, as if he had not known what silence was before. He did not know why he had been arrested and if he did not know why he was here, he would not be released.

He had been having coffee with a student in an apartment when two cops came in. He was taken to DeHoCo, the Detroit House of Correction. A student told him later that he was waiting for a bus when a cop grabbed him.

He was released the next day without understanding why, any more than he understood why he had been arrested and saw tv cameras on the street outside on the street. A microphone was put in front of his face, and he was asked what he would say, what would he do?

Danek found himself in a hallway. The door behind him had shut. He turned the knob, but it would not turn. There was a door at the end of the hallway. The hallway smelled of boiled cabbage and hadn't been

swept. We're waiting for a shipment he hears Marina
say. It will be here tomorrow, if not today.

It had been a long day on the train for Lenka. Thoughts flashed through her head about what the funeral had been like, how she felt about her mother, her brother saying it was time to come home, it was not good for a woman to be away from home, her sister adding that she needed a man, a woman was not a woman without a man.

Thoughts of Marina and the store got in the way. Between the life she no longer had and the one she had now. She was angry only to become anxious the next moment before she was angry once again. She resented what her life had been, did not believe that the one she had now would last, and feared what would happen. If only what was possible was possible. If she no longer feared what was not there. If she no longer feared what was. There could be, there would be, but what she thought got lost in the landscape rushing by.

When Lenka saw a man stocking the cooler with beer bottles, she turned away. The funeral had depressed her. It had been a long day on the train. She was exhausted. When she turned back, he was still there.

At the cash register, Marina did not seem to be aware that he was there. It was nothing she told herself.

Marina needed help and hired someone. Lenka had been thinking about him and it seemed it brought him forward.

Lenka knew it was him. Marina's man. If she did not know he was there, she did not have to say anything. He would not be there. She was afraid to ask Marina about him. She trusted Marina and needed to trust her now. The day Marina came into the store and worked alongside her Lenka felt she understood Marina. It was different now. Marina not only worked for her but had become....

Stop, Lenka told herself. Stop!   Her family taught her not to trust anyone. Whatever her husband said had been a lie, even when he did not lie. A groundswell of doubt, fear and anxiety overwhelmed her, but it would be worse the longer she delayed going into the store.

Marina saw her and came over to Lenka but glanced at the man at the fridge on the way. She asked Lenka how the trip went. It was good to have her back. She missed her. There were no problems in the store. Well, there was Mrs. Dubrovnik, but Lenka knew what it would be. Marina was calm, as if everything was the way it should be. The man looked at them and waited to see what would happen.

You know what funerals are like Lenka said and shrugged. It's good to be back. She asked Marina if there had been any difficulties, had the bills been paid. She swallowed the question she was afraid to ask, but reached out to touch Marina's arm, as if it would reassure her, but pulled her hand back.

Lenka had to order more pork. The man had to sweep the floor. Marina had to make an inventory of what was in storage. Marina had to make sure there were enough potatoes in the bin. Marina had to do this. Marina had to do that. It only stopped when Lenka went to the bank. You'll manage, she said in a tone Marina thought was not pleasant. Marina had not said anything about Danek, but since Lenka had been back, the sight of Danek irritated, if not angered her.

When Marina first saw Danek come into the store she'd been shocked. He was puzzled, confused and did not know where he was. He might have left the room without realizing he had. Yet he had.

Danek should be here. It was time she said something to Lenka. He could help them in the store. It had been busy. Lenka saw Danek to be a threat when she saw him working in the store, but what she imagined about Danek in their room was far more alarming than a silent man sweeping a floor.

It could not be undone, but it was good to see Danek in the store with her. She had worried about him being alone in the room all day. He had been through so much. Bratislava had not turned out the way he expected. If it had not been for her, she did not know how he would manage. He needed her as he had not before.

Lenka was a different matter. She couldn't allow Lenka to keep him out of the store, but when she went to see Lenka last night, the door was locked. Lenka, she said, we need to talk, but she didn't answer. Marina was about to say something more but left without saying anything. She would not beg.

Marina leaned back against the counter while Mrs. Dubensky counted her change to see if she had enough money. She glanced at Danek who was putting cans and packages on shelves. Things would get better, they had to get better, but she could not convince herself.

Scenes from the morning that upset her came back. Mrs. Dubrovnik all but confronted Marina about her past. Lenka told her something had to be done but did not say what it was. After Mrs. Pistanek left, she saw that her hands on the counter were the wrinkled hands of an old woman. Marina covered her mouth with a hand so that she would not cry out.

No one in the store noticed Danek except Marina and a woman she did not know who one day talked to her. The woman would look at him, say something to Marina and point to him. She frowned as if something had made her angry. The next moment she ran a hand over her forehead, as if it was all too much to deal with. Marina listened to the woman, but never said anything. She was afraid the women had seen Danek in Bratislava at a café, walking down a street. At moments she glanced at Danek when she thought the woman would not see her.

Women in long, black dresses and babushkas came into the store with cloth bags. Women in jeans and tank tops. They did not seem to know Danek was there. In Bratislava he'd been noticed whenever he said something, even when he had not said anything, but if he said anything here, no one would pay attention. Danek remembered what it was like when he worked in a car wash. No one knew he was there.

A woman who was overweight and brought a cart into the store reminded Danek of Mrs. Bomba, who lived next door when he was a boy. A thin, dark-skinned young woman in jeans and tee shirt could have been the Italian who lived up the street. A heavy-set, woman whose white hair had thinned so much that she was nearly bald walked with difficulty into the store. It was not his grandmother, but it could have been.

The street where Danek had been born was a neighborhood of immigrants from eastern and southern Europe who had come to America for a better life. Kuciak, who lived down the street, was up at five to work in a butcher's shop at the end of the street. Grosz, across the street, took two street cars on his way to a factory on the east side of Cleveland.

It had been there before he dreamed of a life coaching football and teaching mathematics in high school, as his brothers had, but he had not seen it. It had been there before he understood why his father quit school in seventh grade to go to work and his mother had been taken out of school after third grade and sent two hundred miles away from home to be a servant in someone's house.

It was not until he went to college that he began to understand their lives and realize how far college had taken him away from them, even if it gave him ways to understand them. He was no longer working class, even if at moments he was reminded that he was. His dream of a life coaching football and teaching math was gone. In Detroit he taught working-class students in night classes. In Puerto Rico it was Puerto Ricans who could not get any other education.

It was not until one day in class that Danek heard himself that he knew he had to leave. What he said he could no longer say. When he first said it twenty years ago it meant something. In America it could no longer be said.

In Bratislava he had become aware, slowly at first, then painfully, that what he saw to be a defeat had become the right thing for him to do. Danek put one beer after another in the fridge. He went to the back of the store to get a broom.

Lenka approached Marina to say we had to talk but asked her whether the store needed more cabbage. She approached the man to ask him why he was there but did not know whether he spoke Slovak and turned away without saying anything, pointing to boxes that needed to be moved. Work Lenka told herself. She had to work. Check the cash register, slice pork for Mrs. Pistanek, see if cabbage was fresh. Work would get in the way. Everything would seem normal.

It was how she worked in the last days of her marriage. Yes, she would say, eggplant arrived this morning, while she wrestled with herself about what to do. She had to say something, but she was afraid to say anything. She wanted it to be over--she could no longer stand what it had become--but feared what it would be like after her husband was gone while she wrapped eggplant and wished Mrs. Pistanek or Mrs. Dubrovnik a good day.

She told the Dubensky woman that they had paprika. She had come from Zilina and Lenka wondered where in Zilina she had lived and why she had come to Bratislava but said nothing. Word had it that there had been a man. Lenka smiled, nodded, wrapped pork, counted change for her.

The Italian woman came into the store. Then it was Mrs. Dubrovnik. So, the day passed. She had not slept with Marina since she'd been back. The more she thought about it, the more wrong it had become, but in the middle of the night she would find herself being fucked, her fingers deep inside her, and cry out from a place she did not know that she knew.

It was the man. If he was not here. There was a reason Marina was with him. She assumed they were lovers. She could not understand why he had remained in their room for so long. It was certainly odd, but the thought of him there haunted her. Marina had not said anything other than with Lenka gone she needed help. Lenka feared how it would turn out.

She glanced at Marina who had carried Mrs. Dubensky's cloth bag to the door, but when Marina saw Lenka look at her, she turned away. She had given an apple and tomato to Marina while she was out of work and said next time we'll talk. They no longer talked. They no longer fucked. The apple, it turned out, had a worm in it.

While Marina wrapped asparagus for the Italian woman at the counter, she saw Johanna at the door, as she had seen her the day she left. She wished the Italian woman a good day and turned to see what she needed to do, not wanting to see if Johanna was still at the door.

She never stopped feeling that she had betrayed Johanna, even if she knew what she had done for her. She had been at her side in the hospital after Johanna tried to kill herself. She took Joahnna into her apartment while she recovered. She had been a good friend, but at some point, she was not sure when it was, she was no longer a good friend.

It began when she dismissed Johanna's worry about work. She had not taken seriously her failure to find a man. She wanted her out of her apartment long before she left. When Johanna came back with a man, she had been afraid Johanna would come back and was glad when she left.

She had not seen Mrs. Dubrovnik standing in front of her. She smiled and told Mrs. Dubrovnik that she was sorry, her mind must have been somewhere else, and asked her what she wanted today. After Mrs.

Dubrovnik left, she told Lenka she was taking a break.

It was as if seeing Johanna at the door was telling her that something had to be done. She had avoided talking about Danek with Lenka. She put off talking to Lenka about what they did. She had not been honest with them. If it was not one thing, it was another.

She had done what she could. She worked in the store. She slept with Lenka. She took care of Danek. If she refused Lenka, they would be back out on the street. She never forgot what it was like in the warehouse, after Danek was gone and she could no longer do anything, but she did not question what she did. The wrong thing had been the right thing. It did not make it any less wrong. Johanna would not let her go.

Marina lay flat on her back in bed, her hands folded together on her lap, eyes shut, as if she were asleep, but Danek was convinced that she was not asleep. He asked her if she needed anything, did she want him to bring a blanket, but she did not seem to hear him. He rubbed his eyes, bit his lip and ran a hand down his thigh.

For several minutes he examined the ceiling. He glanced at Marina, looked away. He waited and would wait for the waiting to tell him what to do. The evening seemed to have absorbed what the day had been. Marina remained in the storage room for a long time. The woman had gone out. Danek was left by himself in the store. He did not know what he would do if someone came into the store, but no one did.

Someone was always in the store. It was as if once Marina went into storage and the woman out the door, they had taken everyone who shopped in the store with them. Danek was left with a broom, pork to be put in the freezer, boxes unpacked.

Danek moved around the room aimlessly, taking plates away from the table, pushing the chair back, rearranging clothing in the closet, not understanding why he was doing what he did, but knowing he had to do something. He stopped at the window and for a moment looked out.

What happened to Marina, he thought, had something to do with the storage room. There were reasons why one went into storage rooms and reasons why one left them, but he did not understand why Marina had gone into a storage room as if everything was all right and come out the Marina who lay on a bed, as if she were dead was beyond him.

The day Marina saw him in Paavo's room when he had not been able to take care of himself is the way he sees her now. Danek struggled to remember how he felt then. He had looked at Marina then, as if he did not believe that she was there. Paavo told me he remembers her say, but Paavo was not there. If he had told her, he would have heard him. Eat, you must eat, he hears. When had it been, where? He no longer remembers. It had been. No, it was. Marina, you must remember Marina.

It was morning. The store had not yet opened. Danek had just come in and went over to Lenka, who was sitting behind the counter. His face was dark, as if it cast a shadow over her. She asked him what he wanted, but he shook his head and gave her a note.

Lenka read the note and asked him about Marina. He did not understand what she said but knew *Kedy*, the Slovak word for where he remembered from the guidebook. He pointed to the door at the back of the store and put his hands against the side of his head to say that Marina was sleeping.

Lenka brushed past Danek and went towards the back of the store. She had to see for herself how Marina was. She would not find out anything from this man. Danek got in the way. She looked at him, as if he was not there. A balding, middle-aged man who worked in business or a bank. She never trusted them. They were not her kind.

He was in the way. He was in the way before she ever saw him. *Uz to peckla* she said, but he answered *nie, nie*. It surprised her that he understood her, but she did not know what to do about it. She heard a knocking at the door. She needed to see Marina, but if she did not open the door of the store there would be talk. She pointed to the fridge, as if he would understand

Mrs. Dubrovnik was at the door. Then the woman from Zilina came. And the Italian woman. While Lenka helped them, she would glance at Danek to see if what she saw would tell her something.

Mrs. Dubrovnik asked about Marina. Flu, Lenka said and nervously rubbed her hand over her forehead. She'll be back in a day or two. It's nothing. Lenka knew Mrs. Dubrovnik thought it was something. One day there had been Marina. And one day a man. It was strange. Lenka didn't need help.

Marina, Lenka asked Danek, pointing to Danek and then herself before indicating a third person standing between them. She raised her hands in desperation, as if she did not know where Marina was. Danek shrugged, shook his head, pointed to storage, as if that was where she wanted him to go.

Marina was as much there as she was not there. Lenka was frustrated, if not angry, not certain she could control herself. Danek did not know what he could do. In a way they had not expected they realized what it would be like without Marina.

Where they are is where they were, but the dynamics of it were no longer the same. Marina left for work while Danek stayed in the room, but now it was Danek who went to work and Marina who stayed.

It was as if when Danek came into the store he got stronger, and when she returned to their room she became weaker. He was the Danek she knew but a newer version. She was not sick but did not know why she felt as she did.

It was having to please Lenka, satisfy Danek, defend one against the other and not put herself in between when she had to put herself in between to keep what they had without losing everything that brought about how she felt.

She never knew what happened the night Danek did not come back to the apartment. She was afraid to ask him about it, but whatever happened disturbed him more than it had her. She saw it in his uncertainty, anxiety and even fear. He looked away before he said anything. He would begin to say something but stop, as if he had forgotten what it was.

Why Danek was less himself in the room and more himself in the store had something to do with the room. She had thought being alone all day had not been a problem for him. He wrote in his notebook. He napped. He spoke of a woman he saw in a window of the building across the street.

She had put herself where he had been but did not know what to do. She does not write. She did not want the woman in the window across the alley to see her. She could sleep, but feared what her dreams would be.

The day was there to be taken, but this was different. She should give in to the day, let the room determine what she needed to do. She must let it lead her.

Marina lay back on the bed, closed her eyes, turned over only to turn back. Suddenly she saw the girl on the grass in the Medical Gardens stumble and fall while making a gymnastic move. She rolled over and laughed when she got up. She would try again. The girl had spoken.

In the room a table, chair, bed. Danek sits by Marina before he leaves for work. In the store he does what he is told to do. In storage, he drinks coffee. Danek is there because at a certain moment he has come back. He holds on to what lets him hold on. He will not let it go because without it....

His mother in the market on West 25th Street bargaining over the price of cabbage, gesturing with her hands, pounding a hand against her forehead, switching from Slovak to Hungarian, sometimes German, in the middle of a sentence. Young mothers in long dresses and babushkas, eyes flashing, insistent in their bargaining. The babel of languages and life washed over him.

His father in a pool hall in downtown Cleveland saying your first shot determines what your third shot will be. If it doesn't? For a moment he chalks his cue and looks away. As good as father was at pool, he was never able to play the game of life, although Danek felt his father let it go. He sees himself to be his father's son.

Julie Stevenson standing at the back of a crowd at his birthday party waiting, always waiting, but Danek knew, without having to know, that she did not wait for him. He was not her kind, but waited for her, nevertheless. It was not until much later that he understood that her husband, who was her kind, was not who—what--she wanted. It was as if she had to go where he would not go, before she could free him.

Danek in a grade school classroom, the time he thinks time began, humiliated for saying *pablon*, a word no one knew, but he would not stop saying it in one way or another, however he could, whatever it would be, that it could be said, that he could say it.

Lenka sees herself walking in a field with Marina. There were woods downhill, a pond beyond. The sky was deep blue, the sun high in the sky. Sparrows darted back and forth. In a field a rabbit stopped when it saw them. It was summer, but the mountains were still covered with snow. There could not be any place in the world like it.

Where was Marina?

For a moment Lenka did not know where the question came from until she saw Mrs. Dubrovnik in front of her. Don't get me wrong, she said. It's not Marina. She took in the store with a sweep of her hand. It's me, She laughed. I can no longer shop without Marina helping me.

Mrs. Dubrovnik should ask Lenka not where Marina was but where she, Lenka, was. She was where she should be, but no longer knew where that was. She had moved beyond her Catholic girlhood upbringing but did not know where she was now, if anywhere. She glanced at Mrs. Dubrovnik. In the past she depended on Lenka to help her.

Lenka saw that Danek stopped what he was doing at the mention of Marina's name. Everyone would ask about Marina today. It would be Mrs. Pistanek and then the Matovic girl. Even the Italian woman. No one would want to know where Marina was more than Lenka.

It had something to do with her, but Lenka did not want to think about it. She needed to talk to Marina about them, but the them Marina wanted to talk about were Lenka and Danek. He's here, Marina would say. We work alongside one another. You must accept him

Things would be better if she did, but she felt he would get in the way if she did and he had. She had told her husband she would leave, if he did not stop seeing the other woman, but if she told Danek to leave, Marina would leave. The line had been moved with Marina. She had gone beyond what she could do and would not go any further.

Mrs. Dubensky stood in front of Lenka and asked about tomatoes. Lenka smiled, as if everything was all right, and asked her what kind of tomatoes she needed. There was more than one kind, as if she had not thought about it before.

The price of cabbage was too high, Mrs. Pistanek said. There was no reason for it. She would not say anything about potatoes. It did no good to complain, but she could not help herself. Marina agreed, but it was more than the cabbage she had in mind. Lenka's wrath had come down on her and Danek questioned why she had come back to work.

Wherever she turned it was on her mind. The Matovic girl complained about candy, but Marina remembered Lenka say, it's not right, not right. It was not clear what she meant, but Marina knew it was about her. It did not matter what was said. The Italian woman asked if they ever had pasta and she remembered Danek liked pasta. Mrs. Dubrovnik would come in. Marina did not want to hear what she would say. She took off her apron and put it on the counter. She glanced at Danek on the way out of the store.

That it had come to this. No matter what she did she was up against it. There was nothing to keep her here, but what had put her here in the first place. In the corridor on her way to her room, she stopped. She had a curious, physical feeling, as if she were living in another body, had walked away from herself. Suddenly a memory flashed up and seized hold of her.

Her mother was waiting for her husband to come home, the smell of a woman on him. She was her mother's girl but had not been her mother's girl. It had been her mother who sent her out the door and into the world so that she would not have the life her mother had.

When she saw the door to their room at the end of the corridor, she saw Johanna standing in front of it. Johanna had seen no way to live, but had, nevertheless, chosen to live, no matter how, no matter what it would be. She was there to let Marina know.

There was nothing to keep her here, except Danek and working in the store, but she was no longer sure that she could stand it.

It had been an apple.

Danek picked up an apple and showed it to Lenka. *Cho,* he said. He speaks Slovak Lenka thought, but then realized he can't be Slovak. Anyone who was Slovak would know the Slovak word for apple.

Danek repeated his question. It was not the apple, but what its name would tell him. It was no longer God's apple, but the name Adam gave it. What did Adam mean?

Jablko, Lenka said, thinking she'd humor him. He pointed to a bin of green peppers. She was not sure what he meant, but then he repeated his question, as if *cho* was the only Slovak word he knew. Paprika, she said. If this was a game, she could play it too. She picked up an onion and held it out to Danek.

Cibula.

He knew Slovak. It was no longer a game. He had been playing with her, but she could not guess why he had. She gestured that Danek should go into storage.

It was as if he was making fun of her. He must know some Slovak, but why would he want to know the Slovak word for apple? Those from the West take advantage of us, her husband would say. But she did not know what he had in mind. She was making too much of it but felt there was more to it than she knew.

Marina brought him into the store. What would she do next? Did she have relatives who needed work? Did she want more influence on how the store was run? She could not make any sense of it. What did this have to do with an apple?

She had taken in Marina when she was out of work and living on the street. She could put her out on the street again but knew she couldn't. Everyone liked Marina. They would talk if she let her go. But it would be her, Lenka, who could not let her go.

But Marina was not there. Danek had given her a note saying she was sick. Lenka was not sure what to believe. Marina knew that Lenka did not want him here. Was it a way for Marina to get back at her?

Danek was putting bottles of beer in the fridge. Lenka watched, as if each bottle followed in some order. She saw Marina standing outside the store and then saw Marina in bed with her. Then she saw Danek. Would she fuck him too? She gestured to the man that she was going into the storage room, waved around the store and pointed to the door for him to manage the store while she was gone.

Jablko?

Was that not what Eve offered to Adam? It was not what Danek had given her, but she did not understand what it meant. To make things easier between them? To pass the time of the day?

Marina told Danek to leave and turned to Lenka before she said we need to talk, as if she could not get it out fast enough. It had taken her too long.

For a moment Lenka did not say anything. She bit her lip. She clenched her right hand and then unclenched it. She looked over Marina's shoulder at the door.

--Not now. It's not the time. Someone will be at the door.

Marina went up close enough to Lenka that she could not turn away. It is time. It's long past time. Put a sign up saying we're doing inventory. Lenka turned away, one hand on the counter supporting her. She knew what her husband would do, but Marina was not a customer, and she was not her husband. Marine worked for her. She did not tell Lenka what to do, but Marina had told her, and she had done nothing.

There was a knocking at the door. It would likely be Mrs. Dombrowicz. She was always there first thing in the morning. She told Marina to answer it. It would give her time to think about what she would say, but she had given herself time for some time and not come up with anything to say.

She wanted Marina. She wanted Marina ever so

much, but she was never sure how Marina felt. She could not escape thinking that Marina went to bed with her to keep her job in the store, even if she did not believe it. They got along. She had never had a friend before.

Once she became aware that he was here, she never could acknowledge that Marina had a man. How could he be there, if Marina was with her? She understood, suddenly, as she had not before, that she would have to find another woman if Marina left, although there would never be another Marina. It had not been possible in the first place.

Mrs. Dombrowicz dragged one foot behind her when she came into the store. She had fallen, Marina said. She needed Marina to help her. She lives alone. Marina took her arm, led her through the store and put everything in a bag. At the register Marina said she was taking her home.

Lenka would have done it herself. Mrs. Dombrowicz had been a long-time customer, even if at times it had been difficult. She never asked for help, but the Italian woman spoke of how Mrs. Dombrowicz helped her make her way around the neighborhood when she first arrived.

When Mrs. Dombrowicz left with Marina, Lenka knew it would be a while before she came back. It would be painful for Mrs. Dombrowicz to walk, and they would stop from time to time. She would insist that Marina have tea. Lenka was afraid what Mrs. Dombrowicz would say about her

She glanced at Danek. She did not know what Marina saw in him, but he must be some man if she is with him, although she did not know what it had been. Marina seemed to take care of him.

Lenka left a note for Marina at the register saying she would not be at work today. Marina had told Mrs. Dombrowics that she would stop by today and see how she was. She needed to go to a pharmacy for medication for her. Danek would have to manage the store. He would get by with what little Slovak he knew she thought. He knew what was in the store. Whether he knew the price of any item or could use the cash register was something else. Somehow it would work out.

Marina realized she didn't know how to describe how she felt. She was free. She'd been freed. She remembered nights in their apartment making pierogies, Danek putting together a salad and opening a bottle of wine, enjoying being with Danek, settling down after dinner with *becherovka,* as if they had all the time in the world.

Before she left, she needed to take Danek around the store to make certain he knew where everything was. She would make sure he knew how to use the cash register. Money was a different matter, but he'd been in Bratislava long enough to know what most of the coins were. A Euro was a Euro.

When she took Danek around the store, pointed out

that he should get more cabbage from storage, showed him where there was more money in the drawer of the counter, Marina found herself touching him on the shoulder, even patting him on the ass. It had been some time since she had. It was different now, less about desire than affection.

She never thought it would be this way. She never thought about tomorrow. Tomorrow would come and she would let it come. There would always be something. With Danek it had been today, always today, until there were no longer any more todays. They got by, but it was not what she had in mind.

Danek's life, she knew, had been what he wanted until it no longer wanted him. Marina knew she could no longer live as she once did. She had not thought about what it would be like. She looked around the store. It told her what she did not want to know.

L enka was not there. Marina left to see if Mrs. Dombrowicz was all right. If Danek knew what he did in the store, he did not know what else he needed to do. Marina had explained to him what some of it was, but much of it he did not understand.

Slovaks say *dobry den* when they come into a store and *dovidenia* when they leave. Good day and goodbye endlessly repeated. If he answered them in Slovak, they would think he knew Slovak.

They would expect him to say something. Even the deaf and dumb find ways to make themselves understood, but Danek did not know what he could do to make them understand him. Shrug? Hold out his hands as if he did not know what was asked? Point?

They might have heard him say something to Marina, but he didn't think that they had. He rarely said anything to her while they worked. This morning, they would ask him whether cabbage was fresh, what the price of pork was. He would not know whether it was cabbage, pork or green pepper they meant.

Danek glanced at the broom he held in his hand. The pen he once held in his hand was no longer there. The pen was not a broom he thought, but it needed the broom before it could write.

He remembered the day a man had knocked on the door of his apartment his first day in Bratislava and asked him a question he did not understand. *Nerozumiem po Slovensky* he answered in guidebook Slovak. He didn't understand Slovak. It was all he could say. The man repeated what he said and Danek answered as he had before. It went on in this way until the man left in frustration.

His *Nerozumiem po Slovensky* would not be understood, even if it could not be misunderstood. It distanced himself from them. A distance that could not be overcome no matter how much Slovak he knew. It was a moment of *pablon*. A moment in which he was not one but not the other. A moment in which he would never be them.

Lenka cannot do what she wants, if she even knows what it is, but needs to do what she can't. What about the man? Marina? And most difficult of all, herself, Lenka? What ifs that followed one another in lock step. Wave after wave of them breaking upon the shore of herself and pulling her under. She finds herself grasping for breath.

The man's face pops up in front of her, saying, saying he was here, he would be here. She turns away from him, but his face pops up on the other side, circling around her. This man, him, the one she does not want to see, never wanted to see. The one who should not be there.

She turned over, brought her knees up to her chest, cradled them against her, closed her eyes. She saw Marina standing outside the store, not sure she would come in, but knowing she must. When you come back next time, we can talk she said. It had been talk that brought Marina into the store, into her bed, into a life she did not want to lose.

It was talk that was taking Marina away from her. There had been too much talk. She had never been comfortable with anything that had been said. Talk was never anything but talk. It got in the way. And it had got in the way.

Lenka felt the man against her back, whispering, whispering do the right thing, do the right thing, but it was not the right thing. What has she done Father Bukaj asks. Were there sins that she had committed that needed forgiveness, absolution?

One day on the way home from school she saw a girl go down on a boy and take him in her mouth. One day her husband took her in the ass. It was the woman Father Bukaj knew, not the man. Eve had given Adam an apple. The right thing had never been the right thing Lenka knew. It was not what the Bible says, not what Father Bukaj tells her, not what she knows.

She had worked in the store. Now the store worked for her. She had not been free. She was less free now. She owned the store, but the store owned her. The man who owned the store before her husband committed suicide after his wife left him for another man. Her husband left Lenka for another woman. Lenka, had she lived, had died.

Mrs. Dombrowicz would come in for the service. Mrs. Pistanek would come in. Mrs. Dubensky and the

Volvo woman. The Italian woman. They had come to pay their respects. They would not stay long. A Tesco store had opened several blocks away. Today's bargains had been put on the wall behind the register, traces of a stone age, left unerased, had become cave drawings.

—Church bells woke me.

Mrs. Dombrowicz looked at Marina as if she was not sure who she was. Tightly she gripped a handkerchief in her hand. It was cold. It was always cold. She had come to Bratislava before the war. There was work for her husband in mills. For a moment she looked over Marina's shoulder and took her glasses off. She examined them before she put them back on. He was a good man. For a moment she touched her knee and winced.

--Are you all right?

Marina would get Mrs. Dubrovnik a blanket if she needed one. She waited for her to say something more. Lenka complained that Mrs. Dubrovnik was demanding, but.when Marina walked Mrs. Dubrovnik home, several neighbors stopped them to ask how she was. When they were sick or had any difficulty. Mrs. Dubrovnik was always there.

--She was past the age of all right, but she's ok.

It had been difficult for her when she lost her husband during the war. He had joined the resistance, and she never saw him again. She never knew what happened, whether he'd been killed or captured. It was a time nobody wanted to know what happened. They would not say anything, or if they knew, would say less. There was Father Tiso, but after him no one wanted to remember anything.

--There were nights she did not know how she got through.

She turned her head, as if she heard a voice she recognized. The bed was empty. How can you sleep in an empty bed? She looked at Marina. Marina, would she make tea? That would be nice.

--It's odd, isn't it?

When she left Poprad for Bratislava she had been the first to leave. It was not done then. Now everyone leaves home as soon as they can. Lenka is from Zilina. Bratislava is not what she thought it would be, but she'll never go back to Zilina. Marina, you're here. Why did we come to Bratislava? It's not Paris.

--It's not Poprad.

Marina laughed. She had been away from Opina so long that for a moment she could not remember its name. It would have been a death sentence if she stayed. She glanced at Mrs. Dubrovnick

--I don't think much about what is going on now.

She coughed, took a handkerchief from her dress and spit phlegm into it. It was not life. What Mrs. Dubrovnick said made Marina think of her own. From Opina to Bratislava to London and back to Bratislava again. It was enough, more than enough. She reached over and held Mrs. Dubrovnik's hand.

His day in the store had not gone as Danek thought it would. He had been taken away from himself and brought back by a gesture that at the next moment took him away from himself. It had not been the disaster he feared.

Mrs. Pistanek had come in and asked him about--it could have been oranges or pork--but he did not understand anything she said. He shook his head. She repeated what she had asked. He pointed to cabbage, as if, somehow, that's what her question had been about. She shook her head.

Danek needed to do something and thought if he showed her what was there, she would let him know what she wanted. He walked Mrs. Pistanek down the aisle pointing to carrots, tomatoes, eggplant, potatoes. In this way Mrs. Pistanek found what she needed. She may have been surprised if not puzzled but did not think about it.

Then it was the Volvo woman. Danek knew what she bought because every week it was the same. It was potatoes, not yams. Green peppers, not red, wine, not beer. Before she said anything, Danek took her through the store to pick up what she usually bought, stopping at moments to see if the pepper was fresh, how much the wine cost.

Before someone asked him something he could not answer, the Italian woman came into the store. She had run into Mrs. Pistanek on her way to the store who told her what it had been like shopping in the store today and asked questions about him.

The Italian woman remembered what the Slovak she'd been with in Italy told her about his experience working in Italy. He was there, but he was not there until he did something that made them notice him. After that they would always see him. The life of a *gastarbeiter*, he laughed.

You're not Slovak she said to Danek in German, but he did not answer. When he did not say anything, she asked him in English. For a moment Danek did not say anything. No, he said. He knew he could not explain why he worked here. The Italian woman did not press him about it. It was none of her business.

It would have done Danek no good to say anything. The Italian woman would explain to Mrs. Pistanek that Danek was an immigrant who would let the Volvo woman know. There had never been immigrants before. It was a new world, even if they did not understand it.

They would ask why Lenka needed a guest worker. The store must be doing well, very well for Lenka to hire him, but the store was small and did not have much business. Marina had already been hired. There was no need for him. Their interest would shift away from Danek. He would not be seen as he had not been seen in the first place.

Danek looked around the store. There was cauliflower he had to move, potatoes, cabbage and onions. He had become useful in a way that he had not been as a writer, even, he thought, as a teacher. One of the many who did what they did to get by. An immigrant like his mother

Shadowy, insubstantial outlines fading and soon gone. Then, suddenly, as if a door had been opened, shapes materialize and Lenka sees Danek crouching at the back of the store and Marina at the front door.

Lenka had gone into the store before it opened, a voice telling her go, go into the store, see it, see it as you did not before. Ten years of your life spent there, your youth lost in back-breaking labor, ten years you'll never get back. See yourself with cabbage and potatoes waiting to be bought. See yourself in the fridge sold like beer.

As if it were a dream, Lenka sees Marina at the register finalizing Mrs. Dubrovnick's bill. Danek was bringing eggplant from storage and putting them in a bin. She heard Mrs. Dubrovnick say something to Marina and they laughed.

They're here, she thinks. They come with the store. Lenka went down an aisle away from them, not wanting to hear anything more. She stopped, picked up bananas and examined them, as if everything was as it should be. She picked up a box of blueberries and then an apple. It had been an apple. Everything had begun with an apple.

No, Lenka thinks, no. It began before, long before. The day in Zilina she saw a girl with a boy in an alley. She wanted to be that girl. She was that girl.

--Is that what you had with Marina?

Lenka looked around the store to see who asked. Danek had gone into storage. Marina was opening the front door but had not said anything. Lenka put the apple back in the bin.

What she had with Marina was more than she ever thought it would be. It had been her, Lenka, Lenka herself, who had done it. She told Marina if she came back, they would talk. It had been her talk that brought Marina into the store and into her bed.

Lenka saw Marina walk across the room. She saw Marina unbutton her blouse and step out of her slacks. The door was open. Mrs. Dombrowicz would come in, Mrs. Dubensky would, the Volvo woman. Marina's blouse on the floor, her slacks alongside.

The door was open!

Her days were no longer what they had been. Each day was more difficult than the last. Marina would not live in the past as her mother did, remembering the man she had once loved when she saw the man she despised. But it was the day, this day, that nevertheless needed to be kept, made the most of, however, it could.

Danek worked in the store, swept the floor, stacked bottles and bagged cauliflower, as if he had been put in motion by a life that had defeated him and pushed forward by what was left. It had nothing to do with her, but everything to do with her.

Lenka had saved her until she no longer did. Marina soon realized that Lenka had never been in control of herself and was less in control of herself now. Her problems had always been there, but she did not want to deal with them. What Lenka thought came out whenever she thought about it. What she said could not be put back. It made life with Lenka impossible.

The night she first saw Danek she moved close to him and had been moving closer to him ever since. She had not seen that in growing closer to Danek she had been moving away from herself. She had not seen that she had put herself in Lenka's hands.

There was no taking back what had been taken away. It had been given to Danek and appropriated by Lenka. She was there to take care of Danek, who could no longer take care of himself and Lenka who could not take care of herself.

Danek leaned back against a wall in storage. His back ached. His calves were sore. He could be somewhere else, but it would not be any different. He no longer waited for a somewhere else.

He sees Mr. Jacob at dinner in their home. He had come to America to work and needed a place to stay. He was a distant relative or a friend of a friend from the old country. Mother must have said something.

Mr. Jacob was short, thin, with thick glasses that made his deep brown eyes seem large. His graying hair was receding. He could have been middle-aged. He left for work before Danek was up and went up to his room after dinner. He never went out.

At dinner Mother would ask Mr. Jacob how the food was, but he would never say anything more than good, it was good. He did not say anything about work, what he thought about life in America, how he got along in a foreign country, what life in the old country had been, as if his silence said more than he could say.

There was a woman in the old country Mr. Jacob loved. When he earned enough money, she would come to America, and they would marry. They would have a life in the new country that they could not have in the old. Danek did not know how he knew. It must have been his sister who told him. One day Mr. Jacob was not there. His mother did not say anything.

Danek had put the new world behind him as Mr. Jacob had the old, but it had not turned out as they hoped. It stops there. Somewhere in America there was a Mr. Jacob. Somewhere in Bratislava a Danek.

Lenka told Marina to manage the store on Sunday. She needed to get away. Marina wanted to talk about Danek, talk about them and Lenka had put her off for too long.

It had been some time since she'd been more than a few blocks away from the store. Her husband had taken her to clubs around the SNP Square. The train station where a train took her to Zilina was up the hill from the store.

The day was sunny and warm. Everyone was out to take advantage of the weather and day. Lenka walked wherever she did with no sense of where she went. She was surprised by the number of Chinese, Japanese, Americans--even Germans and Poles--who were in the old town. She had not known there was something called a tour that brought them from all parts of the world. Bratislava had become a world-class city like Vienna or Budapest without Lenka knowing it had. Life had passed her by, as it had, she thought, from the beginning.

There were middle-class neighborhoods Lenka was in, like those around Slobody Square, where she knew she should not be. There were other neighborhoods, particularly those east of the university, on Tallerova, that were like streets in her neighborhood but had a life that hers did not have. Without realizing she had, Lenka had put together her own map of Bratislava.

She stopped at Umelcka, a beer garden near the Slovak Union of Visual Artists, to have coffee. She did not look around, not wanting to see if anyone noticed her. In some neighborhoods where she walked, she was noticed and made to feel that she should not be there.

When the waitress set down a second espresso, Lenka saw the Italian woman at the door. She had not expected to see anyone she knew and for a moment was confused. Umelcka was far from where she lived. Lenka looked around to make sure that she was in the beer garden. Then the Italian woman waved and came over.

They talked, laughed and drank beer. Time passed. The Italian woman knew of a club down a narrow street below the Bratislava Castle that had music. They could dance. The day was there to be taken. So, they went. It did not surprise Lenka that there were only women in the club.

This was, this was.

Marina sees herself in London, a voice saying go home, go back, you are not one of us, you'll never be one of us, you don't belong, you, you Slavic bitch. She hears Lenka's manic, forced laughter. The Italian woman was at the counter talking to Lenka. She sees her smile at Lenka, a smile that only those who knew what it meant would understand. Last night Marina had gone to Lenka's room but left when she heard laughter. She did not belong in London and was beginning to feel she did not belong here.

Danek was at the other side of the store fascinated by Campbell soup cans. He no longer complained that he was not him, himself, whoever thought he was him. It was difficult, if not impossible, to talk to him, as if he had put up a sign saying Do Not Disturb. Mrs. Dubrovnick was not getting better and no longer said anything.

What had been there was no longer there. It was disorienting and made Marina anxious. There was not anything she could say to Danek or Mrs. Dubrovnick. She did not know what she would say to Lenka, but the Italian woman gave her a reason not to talk to

Lenka. She was relieved but felt no relief. It struck her, suddenly, that she was no longer necessary. She who had been necessary to Danek, Lenka, Dubrovnick.

This was the story.

Mrs. Dubrovnick's story was over. Danek's story was still being written and would not stop being written. The story of Lenka and the Italian woman had yet to be written. Marina would not let herself be written out of the story. She went to Danek and put a hand on his shoulder. She went to Lenka, smiled at the Italian woman and told them that she was happy, so happy for them. Her world was closing in on her, but she needed to let it know she was there.

There had become here and then now. Lenka was at the counter talking to the Italian woman. Danek heard the Matovic girl laugh at something Marina said. Mrs. Pistanek examined tomatoes. Mrs. Dubensky had just come into the store. Danek saw them from a distance, as he saw the woman at the window of the building opposite. He never seemed to be there, even when he was there. Something inside him stood outside himself, waiting. A disembodiment.

When he heard the Italian woman laugh at what Lenka said and saw Mrs. Pistanek turn away from the tomatoes, not pleased by what she had seen, Danek realized he could not overcome the difference between them that their lives established. They were not him. He was not them.

We say what we do, he thought, because what cannot be said must, nevertheless, be said, even if it cannot be said. All that remained was the shrug with which doctors signal their failure.

Trish Stevens came to mind. She taught at the university in Detroit that Danek did. Everyone knew she had been in love with her thesis advisor, had her thesis rejected and her teaching contract not renewed.

When she committed suicide by stepping off the bridge over the Detroit River everyone had his story. It was despair they said, an accident, not deliberate. No one would know, but it did not stop them from thinking what they wanted to believe.

Why did he write? Why did he fall in love? Because. There was nothing more to say. Later when asked Danek would say something about his parents, this moment or that, a book he read, someone he met, something that happened, but whatever he said did not explain anything. He had to. Because. Why had he gone to Puerto Rico? Because. A deserted farmhouse in Indiana? Bratislava? Because.

Lenka?

She no longer slept in the store. She was out every night and stayed with the Italian woman. Then she stopped working in the store. Marina heard that she had moved up town with the Italian. She missed her. It was not what Lenka thought would happen, but once it did, she embraced a life she once condemned.

—The grocery store?

One day two men came into the store. One was a lawyer. They were authorized to verify what was there. The store had been sold, in the words of the lawyer, to two Asian gentlemen of dubious background. They would bring in their own staff.

—Danek?

He's gone. It's a blessing. At the end he no longer understood anything. Marina looked down at her hands in her lap. It had been hard for her to see him. *She held his hand and looked at him, remembering what he was like when he was excited by something that was said, how his eyes flashed, and had not seen him go.*

She has his notebook. That's all he left. She won't do anything about it. It's his. That's enough.

—You?

She takes care of Mrs. Dombrowicz. Mrs. Dubensky had an extra room after her son died.

ROBERT BUCKEYE is author of five works of fiction about Puerto Rico (*Pressure Drop*), the Kent State shootings (*Still Lives*), Edvard Munch (*The Munch Case*), Bratislava (*Fade*), and the novel *Not Her Nor Him*, as well as a study of the English novelist, Ann Quin (*Re: Quin*). In 2015, Spuyten Duyvil published a collection of his criticism, *Living In*. *The Grocery Store on Lasaretska Street* is a continuation of *Nightfall*, also published by Spuyten duyvil. He divides his time between Vermont and Bratislava.